Leopard got his Spots

by Rudyard Kipling

Retold by Rosie Dickins

Illustrated by John Joven

Long ago, when the world was new, the leopard lived in a place called the High Plain.

It wasn't the Low Plain or the Medium Plain, but the bare, hot, sunny High Plain. It was full of sand and sandy-brown rock and sandy-yellow grass.

Everyone who lived there was sandy-yellow or sandy-brown too.

Leopard was the most sandy-yellowy-brown of all. He matched the sandy-yellowy-brown plain to the last hair.

This made him **VERY** hard to see. When he was hunting, he could sneak up and surprise the other animals right out of their lives.

Searching for somewhere to hide, Zebra and Giraffe came to a forest.

It was a great, high, tall forest, full of dark blotches
and patches and stripes of shadow.

Zebra and Giraffe stayed in the forest so long,
they grew dark blotches and patches and stripes too.

Now Zebra and Giraffe matched the forest so beautifully, you could only see them if you knew where to look.

Out on the plain, man and Leopard hunted high and low together.

"I'M HUNGRY," sighed the man.

Leopard's tummy grumbled.

"I WANT MEAT!" he growled.

After ever so many days, the two of them came to the forest. They couldn't see much, but...

OOF!

The man walked
into something tall.

OW!

Leopard bumped
into something hairy.

"I've caught a
thing that **FEELS**
like Giraffe,"
shouted the man.

"I've caught a thing that **SMELLS** like Zebra!" Leopard roared back.

They dragged the things into a
clearing – and let go in confusion.
"You **ARE** Giraffe and Zebra!
But **WHY** are you so patchy
and striped and strange?"

“Let us show you,” said Giraffe.
Zebra nodded eagerly.

Giraffe and Zebra turned and walked into the shadows.

ONE,

TWO,

THREE...

They **VANISHED!** Just like that.
Muffled laughter drifted through the leaves.
"Where's your dinner now?" snorted Zebra.

The man rubbed his chin.
"That's a clever trick," he said.
"I think I can do that too."
"HOW?" said Leopard.

"Like this," said the man. He took a shadow and wrapped himself up in it, so that he matched the shadows around him.

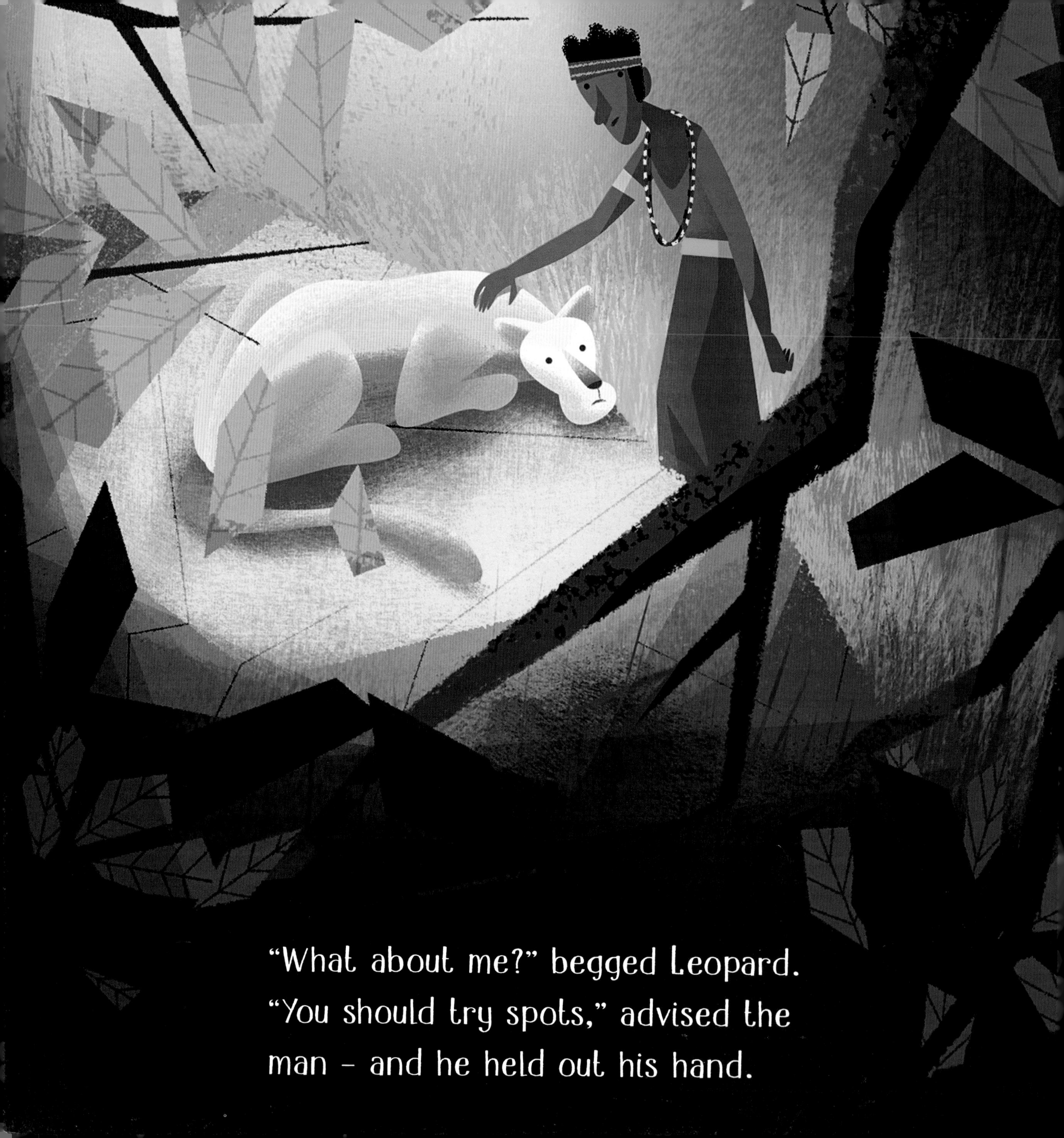

“What about me?” begged Leopard.
“You should try spots,” advised the man – and he held out his hand.

DAB, DAB, DAB! He made shadowy fingerprints all over Leopard's sandy-yellowy-brown fur...

...until it was completely covered in spots.